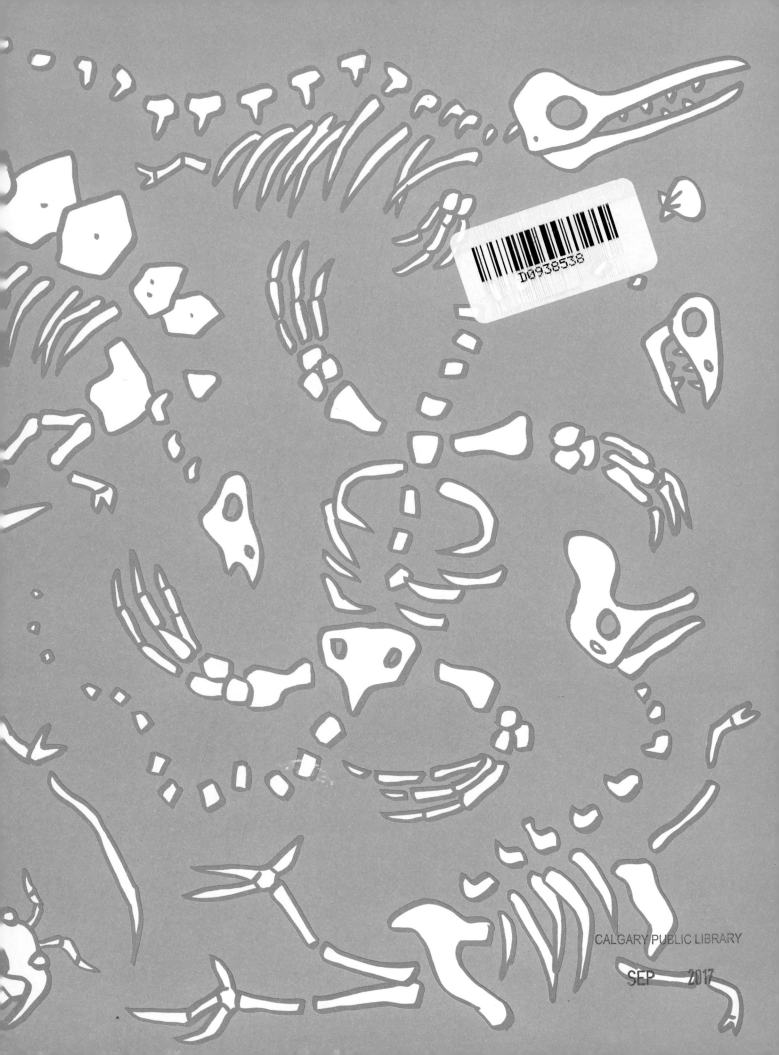

CHICK-O-SAURUS REX

Lenore & Daniel Jennewein

TYRANNOSAURUS REX

Simon & Schuster Books for Young Readers
NEW YORK   LONDON   TORONTO   SYDNEY   NEW DELHI

Every little animal at the farm longed to play in the tree house. Especially Little Chick.

But first he had to face the bullies
who guarded the entrance.

Little Chick clucked, "Can I come in?"

The bullies blocked his way.
"This is a club for the brave
and mighty. First you have to
prove you belong."

Little Chick thought hard.

"My father can COCK-A-DOODLE-DOO!"

"That won't do," they taunted.
"If your father isn't brave and mighty,
you'll never be either."

Back at home, Little Chick squawked in frustration. Who around the coop could teach him to be mighty and brave?

Little Chick paced back and forth, scritching and scratching in the dirt. "Didn't anyone in our family ever do anything brave and mighty?"

Father Rooster nodded his head, wiggling his wattle. "Let me get the photo album, son."

"Our family won prizes, invented the chicken-dance craze, and even . . . crossed the road," Father said proudly.

Great-Grandma

Great-Great-Great-Grandma

Little Chick was not impressed. None of these relatives were brave and mighty. But the last picture caught his eye. "What is Grandpa doing with that bone?"

Great-Great-Great-Great-Great-Grandpa

Grandpa Rooster

"That's a fossil," Father explained. "Legend says that our ancient ancestor lies buried beyond the farm. Grandpa looked for him and I've looked for him but that was the only clue we ever found."

Little Chick couldn't wait to investigate. It looked like a big, mighty bone. "Can we go there? Please? We need to find our ancient ancestor!"

Over the next few weeks, Little Chick helped his father dig lots of holes, looking for more mighty fossils from their ancestor.

Finally they found a promising site!

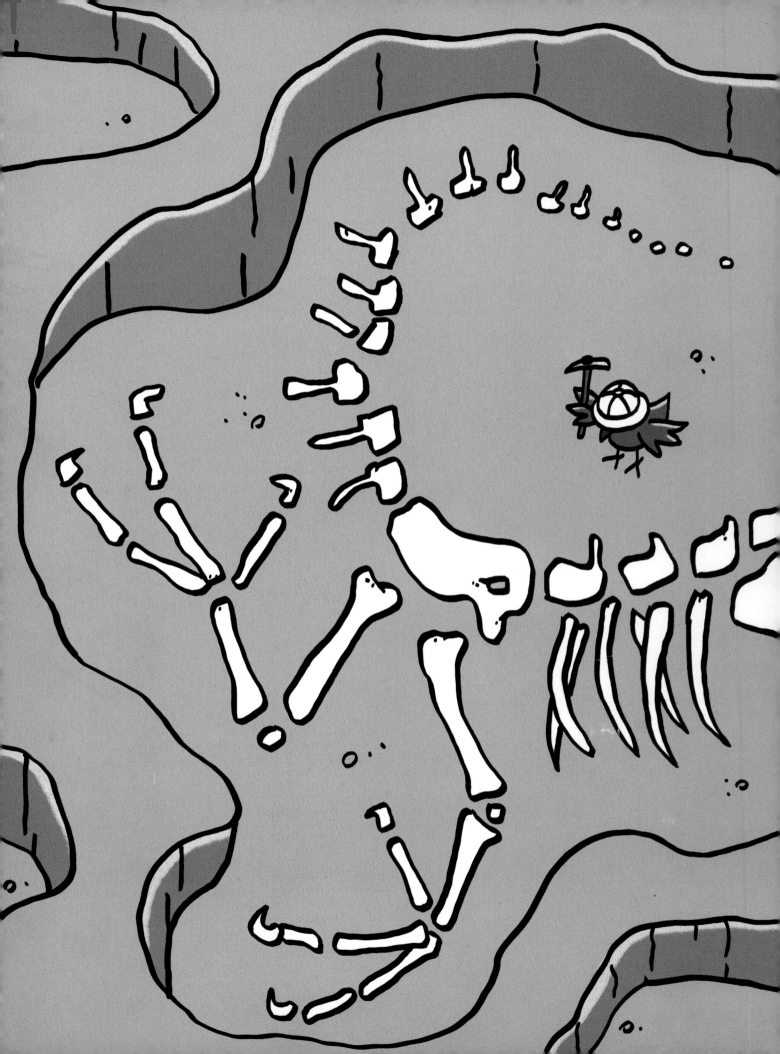

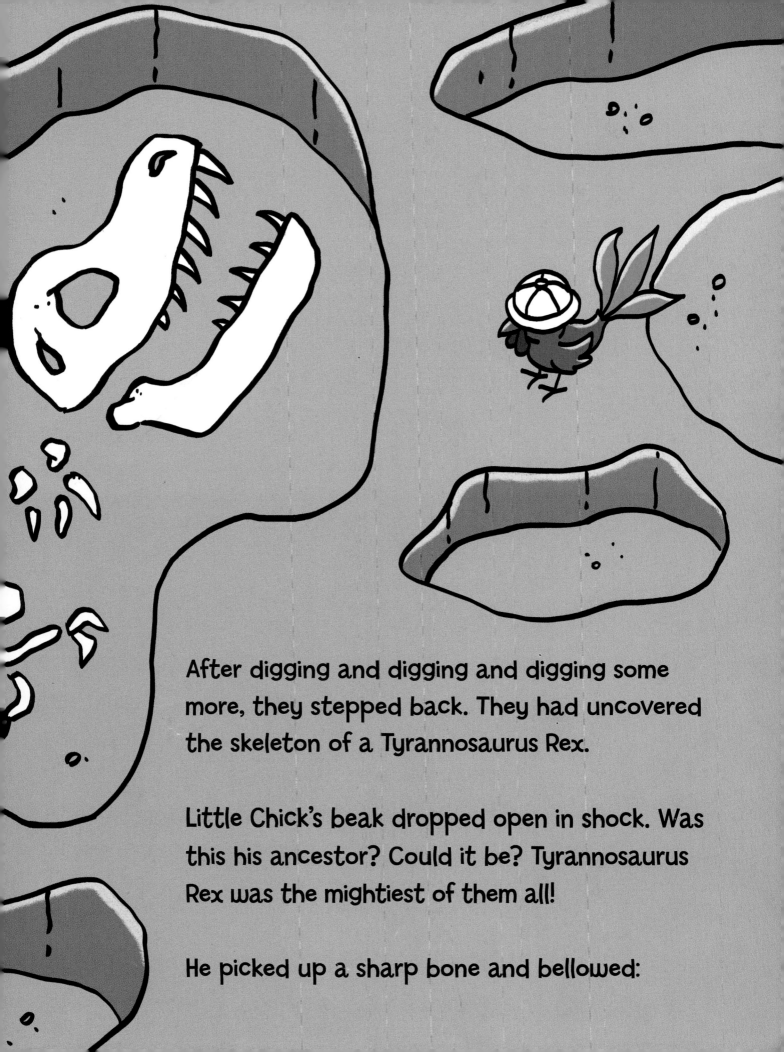

After digging and digging and digging some more, they stepped back. They had uncovered the skeleton of a Tyrannosaurus Rex.

Little Chick's beak dropped open in shock. Was this his ancestor? Could it be? Tyrannosaurus Rex was the mightiest of them all!

He picked up a sharp bone and bellowed:

AM

O-SAURUS

X!

Chick-o-Saurus Rex couldn't wait to tell the bullies that his family was mighty after all.

He swooped and whooped toward the tree house.

He heard the frightened squeals of Little Donkey, Little Sheep, and Little Pig, and the smacking chops of a hungry wolf.

Chick-o-Saurus Rex charged at the wolf, letting out a mighty battle cry.

The wolf didn't know what was happening,
but he wasn't sticking around to find out.

Little Donkey, Little Sheep, and Little Pig had to admit they were wrong. Little Chick had acted very mighty and brave.

The big animals cheered for Chick-o-Saurus Rex. The small animals cheered for Chick-o-Saurus Rex. And from then on, all animals were allowed to play in the tree house.

AUTHOR'S NOTE

Paleontologists (scientists who study dinosaurs) have long known that birds and dinosaurs are closely related. But recently they also confirmed that the chicken is the *Tyrannosaurus rex*'s closest living relative. They did it by comparing trace amounts of collagen protein carefully extracted from an incredibly well-preserved *T. rex* fossil (a bone that has lost most or all of its organic material) with collagen protein from an ordinary chicken bone. So now chickens the world over can brag about their mighty lineage.

For our Jennewein and Appelhans ancestors and relatives, mighty and not

Acknowledgments

A big thank-you to our mighty editor/art director team, Alexandra Cooper and Chloë Foglia, (and the whole S&S team); our mighty agent, Stephen Barbara; and mighty friends with helpful insight and inspiration: Weina Ding, Kirsten Carlson, and Eleanor Mullins.

SIMON & SCHUSTER BOOKS FOR YOUNG READERS • An imprint of Simon & Schuster Children's Publishing Division • 1230 Avenue of the Americas, New York, New York 10020 • Text copyright © 2013 by Lenore Jennewein • Illustrations copyright © 2013 by Daniel Jennewein • All rights reserved, including the right of reproduction in whole or in part in any form. • SIMON & SCHUSTER BOOKS FOR YOUNG READERS is a trademark of Simon & Schuster, Inc. • For information about special discounts for bulk purchases, please contact Simon & Schuster Special Sales at 1-866-506-1949 or business@simonandschuster.com. • The Simon & Schuster Speakers Bureau can bring authors to your live event. For more information or to book an event, contact the Simon & Schuster Speakers Bureau at 1-866-248-3049 or visit our website at www.simonspeakers.com. • Book design by Chloë Foglia • The text for this book is set in Billy. • The illustrations for this book are rendered digitally. Manufactured in China
0513 SCP
10 9 8 7 6 5 4 3 2 1
Library of Congress Cataloging-in-Publication Data
Jennewein, Lenore. • Chick-o-Saurus Rex / Lenore Jennewein ; illustrated by Daniel Jennewein. — 1st ed. • p. cm. • Summary: Little Chick does not feel very brave and mighty until he learns that he is descended from the fierce Tyrannosaurus rex. • ISBN 978-1-4424-5186-5 (hardcover: alk. paper) • [1. Chickens—Fiction. 2. Tyrannosaurus rex—Fiction. 3. Dinosaurs—Fiction. 4. Courage—Fiction.] I. Jennewein, Daniel, ill. II. Title. • PZ7.J42974Ch 2012 • [E]—dc23 • 2012019834 • ISBN 978-1-4424-5189-6 (eBook)

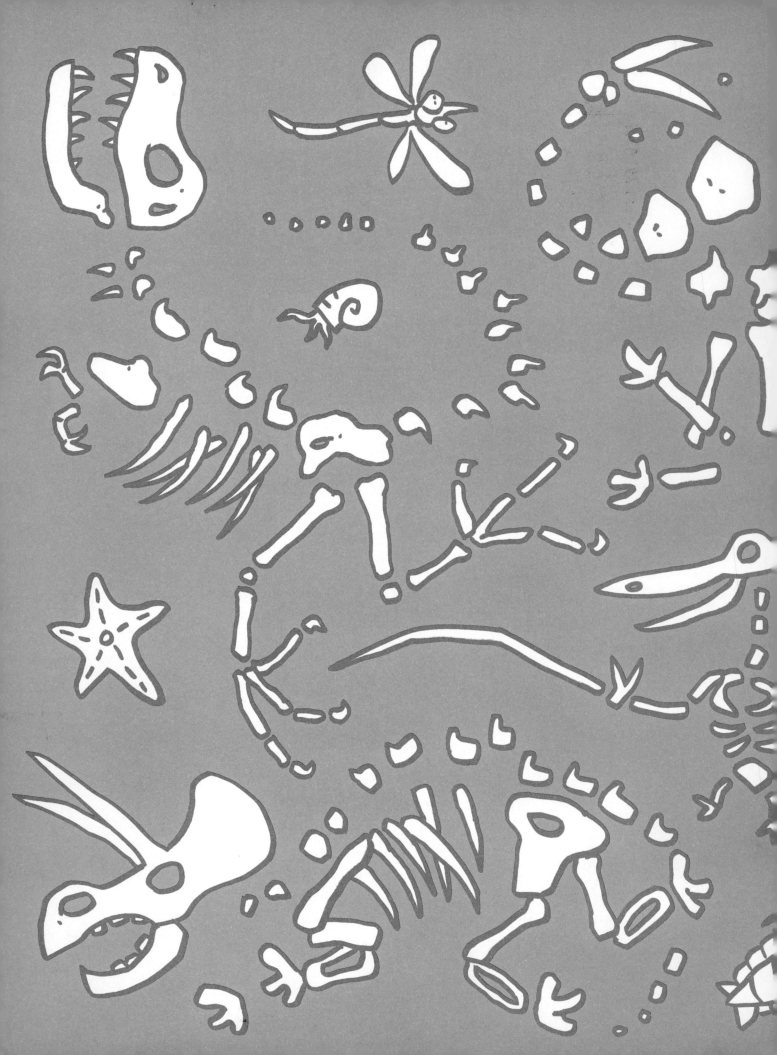